H8382s

SCARED SILLY

A HALLOWEEN TREAT

HAROLD & CHESTER

IN

SCARED SILLY

A HALLOWEEN TREAT

JAMES HOWE

Illustrated by

LESLIE MORRILL

Morrow Junior Books / New York

With love to my daughter

ZOE

born in the Year of the Rabbit

Text copyright © 1989 by James Howe
Illustrations copyright © 1989 by Leslie Morrill
All rights reserved.
No part of this book may be reproduced or utilized
in any form or by any means, electronic or mechanical,
including photocopying, recording or by any information storage and retrieval system,
without permission in writing from the Publisher.
Inquiries should be addressed to
William Morrow and Company, Inc.,
105 Madison Avenue,
New York, NY 10016.

Printed in the United States of America.
1 2 3 4 5 6 7 8 9 10

Library of Congress Cataloging-in-Publication Data
Howe, James .
Scared silly : a Halloween treat / James Howe ; illustrated by
Leslie Morrill.
p.   cm.
Summary: The Monroes leave their cat and two dogs alone on
Halloween night, unaware that their pets are about to be visited by
a strange figure who might be a wicked witch.
ISBN 0-688-07666-1. ISBN 0-688-07667-X (lib. bdg.)
[1. Halloween—Fiction.   2. Witches—Fiction.   3. Dogs—Fiction.
4. Cats—Fiction.] I. Morrill, Leslie H., ill. II. Title.
PZ7.H83727Sc   1989
[E]—dc19   88-7837
CIP
AC

A Note to the Reader

The story you are about to read is told by a dog. But Harold is no ordinary dog. He has written other books about his family, the Monroes, and about his friends—Chester, a cat; Howie, a dachshund puppy; and Bunnicula, a most unusual rabbit.

When Harold sent this story to me, he enclosed the following note:

Halloween is usually a lot of fun at our house. The Monroes really get into the spirit of things with homemade costumes and decorations—and yummy treats! I could hardly wait. But this Halloween was different. Oh, the costumes and the jack-o'-lantern and the candy were the same. But something new was added: a real reason to be scared. I still get goose bumps (or are they ghost bumps?) when I think about it.

I hope my story won't keep you awake at night. But if it does, just remember: even scary stories can have happy endings.

I liked Harold's story, but it didn't scare me so much that I couldn't sleep. After all, it's *only* a story. Besides, I always sleep better with the lights on. Don't you?

—THE EDITOR

All day long the sky had been crawling with clouds as mean and restless as ghosts on the prowl.

"There's going to be a storm tonight," Chester predicted, as Mrs. Monroe called us in to dinner. "And we'll be all alone in the house. Who knows what might happen."

"What do you mean?" Howie asked.

Howie was only a puppy, and I didn't want Chester scaring him, so I said, "He means we might get sick to our stomachs if we eat too many treats."

Howie looked at Chester. Chester looked at me. "Something like that, kid," he said. Howie gulped.

"Nice going, Chester," I muttered over my food dish. "You just had to frighten him, didn't you?"

"Well, it *is* Halloween, Harold."

"I've heard about H-H-Halloween," Howie stammered. "That's when the goblins come out to play. And the witches. And the ghosts and the ghouls."

"Don't forget the skeletons," said Chester. "They'd be hurt to the bone if you left them out."

Howie darted from the room, his toenails clicking madly on the linoleum while Chester chuckled.

"Very funny," I said.

"Oh, come on, Harold, don't be such a party pooper. Being scared is what Halloween is all about."

"I guess you're right," I said, remembering the harmless scares of
Halloweens past.

I looked around. It seemed like an ordinary enough Halloween.

Mr. Monroe was busy carving a jack-o'-lantern.

Toby and Pete were fighting because they didn't want to have to go trick-or-treating together.

"You walk too slow," Pete told his younger brother.

"You run ahead and try to lose me," Toby said.

"Boys!" said Mrs. Monroe, who was rushing to finish the costumes she and Mr. Monroe were wearing to a party that night.

Bunnicula was sleeping in his cage. I knew he would wake up once it was dark, and I wondered if he was looking forward to Halloween. After all, since he is a vampire rabbit—at least, Chester says so—I imagined Halloween might be a special night for him.

I didn't think much about it, though. Eating always makes me drowsy, and it wasn't long before I was sound asleep.

By the time I woke up, it was dark outside. The Monroes were gone. The wind was howling. The windows rattled. The doors and Howie shook.

"What a racket!" he cried. "What's going on?"

"Oh, nothing," Chester said, with a yawn. "Just some creaking bones."

"It's the storm," I told Howie, giving Chester a dirty look.

Howie jumped up onto the sofa and gazed out the window. "Who are they?" he asked.

"Goblins looking for puppies to munch," said Chester.
"Kids in costumes," I explained. "They're trick-or-treating.
Look, Howie, Chester is just trying to frighten you.

That's the fun of Halloween: being scared. But there's nothing really to be frightened of."

There was a gust of wind...

and all the lights went out.

"Except maybe the dark," I added in a tiny voice.

The three of us huddled by the sofa, looking around at the eerie shadows cast by the jack-o'-lantern's light. From across the room, Bunnicula stared at us, his eyes gleaming, his teeth glistening, his shadow making him seem twice as big as usual. There was something in the way he looked at us that held us spellbound.

We ran behind the big brown velvet armchair. Howie was
cowering there already, panting rapidly.

"Who-who-who's at the door?" he asked.

"The wind," I answered.

The door flew open.
"Uncle Harold," Howie said.
"Yes?"
"Does the wind wear a hat?"

There before us, not ten feet away, stood a witch.

"What a night!" she said, her voice so rough it seemed full of gravel. She dropped a bag on the floor, rubbed her hands...and the door slammed shut!

The witch came toward us, but stopped when she reached the jack-o'-lantern. In its light we could see her long, crooked nose; the hairy warts on her wrinkled cheeks; the spider dangling from her hat.

"Help!" Howie yipped.

"What was that?" snarled the witch, turning her head.

"Quiet!" Chester said to Howie. "Do you want to end up as a Halloween treat?"

The witch's eyes darted all about. Then she shrugged and carried the jack-o'-lantern off to the kitchen.

We didn't move. We hardly dared breathe.

"What is she doing here?" Chester asked. "Why would she pick *our* house? There's only one reason I can think of." I followed his eyes.

"Bunnicula?"

"The vampire rabbit and the witch. They're in cahoots, don't you see?"

"I thought we lived in Centerville," said Howie.

"Cahoots isn't a place," said Chester. "It means they're cooking something up together."

We heard the sound of pots and pans in the kitchen. "Maybe it's fudge," I said hopefully.

"And maybe it's a witch's brew," said Chester. "Follow me."

We crept across the living room floor and nudged the kitchen door open with our noses. What we saw made us gasp.

Burning candles filled the room. Something was bubbling in a huge pot on the stove. "I was right!" Chester said. "She's concocting a witch's brew." In a voice that crackled and croaked, the witch sang a strange melody as she stirred the pot. "Spells," Chester mumbled. "Chants," Chester grumbled. "Bubble, bubble, toil and trouble!"

All of a sudden, the witch stopped singing. She stopped stirring. She lifted her nose in the air and asked, "Now where are those animals?"

I never imagined that the three of us could fit behind the sofa at the same time, but no one stopped to measure.

"My mother didn't raise me to be an ingredient," Chester said. "We've got to get out of here!"

The kitchen door opened wide. Light poured into the room. The witch was clicking her tongue, calling for us, her head turning this way and that. And then she saw something. "Ah, Bunnicula!" she said.

She lifted the rabbit out of his cage and disappeared with him into the kitchen.

"We've got to save him!" said Howie.

"We've got to save *us*!" Chester said. "We might be next. The only way out is the pet door. We're just going to have to get past her."

"Don't worry," I told Howie. "I'll save Bunnicula."

Slowly, silently, we made our way toward the kitchen door. We
pushed it open and...

"Oh, my stars!" cried the witch, throwing her hands and Bunnicula into the air.

The bunny landed on my back. The witch laughed. Howie smacked into a table leg. Something fell to the floor with a crash.

We almost made it. But just as we reached the back door, it opened and suddenly...

two horrible creatures blocked our way!

As fast as we could, we dashed to the front door and...

monsters even more horrible than the first stopped us in our tracks!

"We're trapped!" Chester moaned, as the creatures gathered around us. "Doomed! Surrounded by hideous—"

Monroes!

The lights came on.

"Mom!" the skeleton cried. "What a surprise!"

"Grandma!" shouted the beast with three eyes, two of which I recognized as Toby's.

"You weren't supposed to come until tomorrow," said the mummy who sounded a lot like Pete.

"I thought I'd arrive early and surprise you," the witch said. "You know Halloween is my favorite holiday."

"Your costume is great," said Mr. Monroe. "But what's wrong with your voice?"

"Oh, I have an awful cold. And to think I traveled here in this storm! And then, just as I got to the house, the power went out. Well, I began to wonder if I wasn't a little crazy to have come at all. I brought Bunnicula into the kitchen to keep me company while I made some hot cider. And the next thing I knew—"

"Cider!" said Toby. "Let's have some!"

There's nothing like a little hot cider and some doughnuts to help you get over the jitters. Howie and I were beginning to relax at last and enjoy Halloween, even though Chester wasn't convinced the old lady was who she seemed to be.

" I know she looks a little like Mr. Monroe's mother under that costume and makeup," he said. "And she sounds a little like Mr. Monroe's mother under that scratchy voice. But she could be a *witch* pretending to be Mr. Monroe's mother. Couldn't she?"

"Nonsense," I said.

"Stop trying to scare us," said Howie.

"By the way, Mom," Mr. Monroe said just then, "how was your flight?"

"A little bumpy. But I still say flying is the only way to travel."

"Flying?!" Howie gasped.
"I was right!" Chester cried.

I didn't know whether Chester was right or not. But I wasn't taking any chances.

"Move over, you two," I said. "It's going to be a long night."